Look out for more
MAGIC MOLLY books:

The girl who talks to animals

Magic Molly

The Clever Little Kitten

HOLLY WEBB
Illustrated by Erica Jane Waters

■SCHOLASTIC

First published in the UK in 2012 by Scholastic Children's Books
An imprint of Scholastic Ltd
Euston House, 24 Eversholt Street
London, NW1 1DB, UK
Registered office: Westfield Road, Southam, Warwickshire, CV47 0RA
SCHOLASTIC and associated logos are trademarks
and/or registered trademarks of Scholastic Inc.

Text copyright © Holly Webb, 2012
Illustration copyright © Erica Jane Waters, 2012

The rights of Holly Webb and Erica Jane Waters
to be identified as the author and illustrator of this
work have been asserted by them.

ISBN 978 1 407 13176 4

A CIP catalogue record for this book is available
from the British Library.

Printed and bound by CPI Group (UK) Ltd, Croydon, CR0 4YY
Papers used by Scholastic Children's Books are made
from wood grown in sustainable forests.

1 3 5 7 9 10 8 6 4 2

This is a work of fiction. Names, characters, places,
incidents and dialogues are products of the author's imagination
or are used fictitiously. Any resemblance to actual people,
living or dead, events or locales is entirely coincidental.

www.scholastic.co.uk/zone
www.holly-webb.com

For Tom, Robin and William

Chapter One
Sparkly Whiskers

Molly sat at the kitchen table, staring sleepily into her cereal. She was tired, but she was smiling. She had a feeling that today was going to be a good day. She gave an enormous yawn, and giggled.

It was still dark outside. Molly really hadn't wanted to get out of bed, but Kitty, her little sister, had been riding an imaginary horse up and down the landing, and the horse kept stopping to neigh loudly outside Molly's bedroom door. Kitty liked someone to play with.

"Why are you so sleepy, Moll?" Dad asked. He looked tired too, but that was because he'd been called out to one of the sheep farms in the middle of the night, for an early lambing.

2

"Kitty woke me up…" Molly yawned hugely again, and tried to remember the dream she'd been having. She couldn't remember exactly what it had been about. Just that it was special.

She leant her chin on one hand and nibbled some more cereal. Usually, when Molly had a dream that felt important, it meant that something exciting was going to happen.

Molly smiled to herself, licking her spoon thoughtfully. Perhaps she was going to meet another magical animal. It felt so long since she'd helped a shy little piglet called Mouse. She'd missed that wonderful feeling of magic swirling around her.

Molly closed her eyes, hunting for any wisps of her dream that might be floating around. What sort of animal had she been dreaming about? Did someone need her help?

"Moll-eee! Look!" Kitty demanded. "I made a dragon out of my toast!"

At the exact same time, the phone rang loudly.

Molly jumped, and just managed to catch her cereal bowl before it tipped into her lap. All the last little bits of her dream went straight out of her head. Except for something to do with whiskers...

Molly's mum got up to answer the phone and her dad gulped his tea in a hurry. At this time of the morning, it was probably an emergency vet call.

"Oh, hello, Janie. Oh no! Yes, you'd better bring her over, poor little thing. Yes, I'll tell Sam and he'll meet you at the surgery in a few minutes." Molly's mum looked sad as she put the phone down. "That was Janie. You know William's mum? They got a kitten just a couple of days ago, and she's had an accident. Janie's going to bring the kitten over to the surgery straight away."

"What's happened?" Molly asked anxiously. She really hoped it wasn't a serious accident. She loved living right next to her dad's surgery, and being able to visit all the animals, but sometimes it could be sad.

"She's trapped her tail, apparently. I'm not sure how it happened."

Molly made a face. William was a friend of Kitty's from nursery. Kitty loved him, because exciting things always seemed to happen when he was there. Like the nursery's giant snails somehow escaping from their tank, and trailing slime all across the new whiteboard.

"William's got a kitten?" Kitty asked, wide-eyed. "I want a kitten!"

Molly sighed. She would love a kitten too. But Mum and Dad thought she and Kitty weren't old enough to be responsible for a pet. If William had accidentally hurt his new kitten, it would just make Dad even more sure he was right.

Molly's dad picked up his cereal

bowl and drank the milk out of it, while Kitty glared at him. Mum told her off for that. "Sorry. Got to rush!" he explained. "And only dads are allowed to do that, Kitty!"

Kitty was all set to argue, but Dad had gone, heading across the yard to the old barn that had been converted into Larkfield Farm Vets.

"I hope the kitten's OK," Molly said, staring after him worriedly.

Her mum gave her a quick hug. "You can go over to the surgery after school to see. We need to get going now, though. We'd better hurry."

Kitty picked up Molly's cereal bowl and drank the milk out of it,

then smiled sweetly at their mum.
"I'm just hurrying like Daddy!"

Molly hurried home after school
with Grandad. Molly's mum worked
as a nurse at the vet's surgery too
and did a lot of the office work, so

9

Grandad quite often helped out with looking after Molly and Kitty. Mum had told them that she needed to do lots of work on the surgery website today.

"I really want to go and see how the kitten is," Molly explained, as Grandad called after her to slow down. "Did Mum say anything about her? A kitten with a hurt tail, who came in this morning?"

Grandad shook his head. "Sorry, Molly, no one mentioned it. We're nearly home, just slow down for a bit. We can't keep up with you – my legs are too old and Kitty's are too short!"

But Molly wasn't listening. She

was wondering if the whiskers in her dream were kitten's whiskers...

"Hi, Molly!" Jenny, one of the nurses, glanced up from the computer. "Come to help out?"

Molly leaned on the counter, looking hopefully at Jenny. "Jenny, is the kitten OK? Dad rushed off this morning because there was a kitten who'd been in an accident."

Jenny smiled. "She's not too bad.

Mrs Warren was worried that her tail was broken, but it was just badly bruised. Your dad's kept her here today just to make sure she wasn't too shocked, but Mrs Warren's going to pick her up later."

"Oh, good!" Molly felt her shoulders relax again – she hadn't realized how much she'd been worrying about the kitten. "What happened to her, anyway?"

"Believe it or not, she got her tail shut in the door of the washing machine!" Jenny shook her head.

"Do you think it was anything to do with William?" Molly asked, anxiously.

Molly's dad put his head round

the door of the surgery. "I thought I could hear you, Molly. Actually, I've a feeling it wasn't William's fault at all – his mum was very upset about it. Come and see the kitten. She's called Posy."

He beckoned Molly after him, into the ward where they kept animals who needed to stay and be cared for.

The ward was almost empty, with little rustling noises coming from just one cage. Molly moved over towards it quietly, not wanting to scare the kitten.

But as she came closer to the cage, Molly realized she needn't have worried. Most cats at the vet's looked miserable – either they were feeling ill, or they just hated being shut away somewhere that wasn't home and smelled all wrong.

This kitten was positively bouncy. She looked up at Molly with huge green eyes, and her silvery whiskers sparkled with excitement.

"Oh! Who are you? Do you belong here? Can you get me out of here, please? It's not very interesting in this cage, and I can hear people talking outside. I'm sure it's much more fun out there. What's your name? Is that nice man your father? You smell the same, did you know? Why aren't you saying anything? You can hear me, can't you?"

Chapter Two
A Magic Kitten

Molly laughed, and Dad joined in.
"She is cute, isn't she? Bouncing
around the cage like that."

But the kitten stared at her crossly.
"What are you laughing at?"

Molly tried to stop giggling,
but the kitten was so funny, and
of course, with her dad there, she
couldn't explain.

"Sam! Phone call for you!" Jenny

was calling from the reception area, and Molly's dad turned to go. "You can get her out, Molly, if you're careful with her tail. Back in a minute."

Molly waited for the door to

swing shut behind him before she turned back to the kitten's cage. "I'm sorry I laughed. It was just that you asked so many questions, I couldn't have got a word in! I can't talk to you in front of my dad, anyway. He's a brilliant vet, but he doesn't understand about magical animals. And he definitely doesn't know that I can talk to them."

Molly slipped the catch on the wire door and opened it carefully. "Would you like to come out?" she asked, her voice very polite.

Posy gave a dignified little nod and allowed Molly to lift her out of the cage. She was obviously trying not to ask any more questions, but

Molly could see
her ears twitching
back and forth and
sideways, it was so
difficult for her to
be quiet.

As soon as she
was snuggled up
against Molly's
chest, she shook
her head crossly.
"Oh, I can't not
ask! Why is it that
you can hear me
talking and no one else can? Who
are you? Are you a witch?"

Molly shook her head. "No. I have
met a witch, though. And my dad

always says I've got a magic touch with animals — he doesn't know that it's really true!" She stroked Posy's delicate little ears, which were still twitching excitedly. "Are you a witch's kitten? You must be magical, or you wouldn't be talking to me, but you don't feel the same as Sparkle, the witch's kitten I met before."

"I don't belong to a witch. But I do have a bit of magic. Look, I'll show you!" Posy closed her eyes tightly, so that they were just little dark slits in her furry face.

Her whiskers suddenly lost their pretty curved shape, and stuck out straight on either side of her nose. She looked as though she were blowing herself up like a balloon.

"Don't hurt your tail!" Molly said quickly. She could see the fur on either side of the neat bandage sticking up too.

"I won't!" Posy gasped. Little silvery sparkles were running along the ends of her tabby fur. "Oh! It still doesn't work!"

"What doesn't?" Molly asked curiously.

Posy sighed and opened her eyes. Her fur smoothed itself down and her whiskers drooped a little. "I don't know. I'm supposed to be able to do *something*, I know I am. But I'm not sure what. I can fluff up and go all glittery, but that isn't very useful, is it?"

"It looked nice," Molly told her, trying to be encouraging. But she could tell from the way Posy wrinkled her nose that that wasn't good enough.

"My mother is a witch's cat and she can do all sorts of things," Posy muttered. "Just being fluffy isn't what I call magic."

"You can talk too," Molly pointed out. "That's magic. In fact, I don't think I've ever met a kitten who talked so much."

"Really?" Posy asked in a hopeful voice. "Oh well, I suppose that's good. What did Sparkle do? The kitten you met before?"

"He was only starting to learn magic," Molly explained. "I don't think he was especially good at anything yet. He did help me make a spell to find his owner – he was lost, you see. He belongs to a witch who lives in the woods, not far from here."

"I *never* get lost," Posy told her. "I always know where I am." She sighed. "But tabby fur isn't very good for witching. Plain black is better, or perhaps silvery, or even white. Tabby is terribly boring." She glanced sideways at Molly as she said this, as though she was hoping Molly might not think so.

"Tabby isn't boring at all," Molly said quickly. "Tabby's clever! Like, like a tiger! It's camouflage. All your beautiful stripes help you hide, in case you need to watch somebody." Molly wasn't sure it would be a good idea to mention hunting. People sometimes brought mice and gerbils to the vet, and she didn't want Posy to start stalking anybody's pet.

The kitten's whiskers curled up
a little, and her eyes sparkled with
interest. "I am very good at watching
people," she agreed. "I always know
things. I like the idea of being clever."

Molly nodded, and then she heard
footsteps. "Sshh! I think my dad's

coming back."

The door opened and Molly's dad beckoned to her. "Janie's come to pick up their kitten, Molly. Do you want to bring Posy through?"

"I'll come and talk to you again soon," Molly whispered in Posy's ear as she went over to the door.

"Oh, look at her poor tail..." A dark-haired lady came forward, looking anxious. "Hello, Molly. I was really looking forward to showing you and Kitty our new pet, and so was William, but not like this." She bit her lip as she stared at the bandage wrapped round Posy. "Will her tail be all right?"

"It should be fine. It's really only

bruised," Molly's dad explained. "She was lucky, though; it could have been a lot worse."

Janie sighed. "I know. Thank goodness she *is* lucky. They do say cats have nine lives, but Posy must have used up most of hers by now. We've only had her a couple of days, and she's been into everything! She fell into William's bath on her first day with us. We didn't even realize she could climb the stairs to the bathroom!"

The water was all sparkly, and there were bubbles! Posy whispered in Molly's head. *I only wanted to see it better. . .*

Molly stroked her ears and then

27

passed her over to Janie, who cradled her anxiously.

"Poor little Posy! I think she must have been trying to see what was inside the washing machine this morning, and I just closed the door without really looking. I feel awful about it and William was so upset."

Molly nodded. She could imagine.

William was a bit naughty, but he was very sweet too, sometimes. And she knew he'd been desperate for his family to have a pet. Molly gave a little sigh. She wished Mum and Dad weren't so strict about pets. Dad said he saw so many animals that hadn't been looked after properly, and he thought Molly and Kitty needed to be a bit older.

Molly was doing her best to change his mind by helping out at the vet's. Mum and Dad had even let her look after a rabbit for a few days, which had been wonderful.

Mostly wonderful... Snowdrop was a magician's rabbit and she kept accidentally disappearing at the just the wrong time. She'd got Molly into a bit of trouble...

Now Molly looked curiously at Posy, as Janie gently put the kitten into the travel cage she'd brought. The little tabby cat was right. Her magic had to be for *something*.

Molly decided that she and Posy had better find out exactly what – before Posy got herself stuck somewhere even more dangerous.

Chapter Three
Molly's Promise

Molly and her dad waved Janie off, and Molly headed back across the yard to the house to do her homework.

"Tell Mum I'll be back over for tea as soon as I've finished the surgery!" Dad called after her.

"How was William's kitten?" Mum asked, as Molly came into the kitchen. Grandad was sitting having a cup of tea with her.

"Posy's OK. That's the kitten's name. She's just got a bit of a sore tail. It didn't seem to be bothering her very much." Molly smiled to herself. Posy hadn't actually mentioned her tail at all, but she could hardly tell Mum and Grandad that.

"Why can't we have a kitten?" Kitty asked, looking up from the picture she was drawing. "Look! I did a kitten picture." Everyone looked at the piece of paper, and then craned their necks to peer at it from another direction. The entire page was covered in pink and green squiggles.

"Very nice," Mum said, smiling.

"But you know why we don't want to have a kitten or a puppy, Kitty. You're a bit young. When you're bigger."

Kitty moaned grumpily, until Mum distracted her with choosing the vegetables for tea, but Molly didn't say anything. There wasn't much point, but she couldn't help thinking that  Mum and Dad always said that. But they never said exactly how *much* bigger.

★

Mum and Kitty picked Molly up from school the next day. As Molly came out of her classroom with her best friend, Alice, a small figure in a bright pink raincoat and wellies shot across the playground and thumped into her stomach.

"Ow, Kitty. . ." Molly moaned, when she had enough breath back. "What's the matter?"

"We're going to tea with William!" Kitty shrieked, grabbing Molly's hand and starting to pull her across the playground. "He's got a kitten!" she told Alice. "Molly has to go now! Bye!"

Alice waved, laughing, as Molly was dragged to the gate. Luckily she'd taken her wellies to school too, as Kitty didn't bother going round the puddles.

"See you tomorrow!" Molly called back. "Are we really going to tea with William?" she asked Mum, as Kitty grabbed Mum's hand too and hurried them down the street.

"Yes, Janie called earlier. William really wants to show Kitty his new pet."

Molly nodded. She was really keen to see Posy herself. She'd been trying to think of ways to help the little kitten find out what her magic was for, but so far she hadn't had any brilliant ideas.

William and his parents lived in a

little row of cottages further down
the road from Molly's house and the
surgery. As they got there and Kitty
wrestled with the front gate, Molly
spotted Posy
in the front
window. She
was sitting
on the sill
next to a vase
of flowers,
obviously
watching out
for them.

"Oh look!" Kitty squeaked with
excitement. "The kitten, the kitten!"

Posy stared wide-eyed at Kitty,
who was jumping up and down.

Then she glanced at Molly, looking slightly worried. Molly smiled at her. Posy was thinking what she was thinking – that Kitty and William together could be a dangerous combination. She stood up, rather quickly, as Kitty ran to ring the doorbell.

Molly could hear feet thundering down the hallway, and there was a rather loud crash. She peered back at the front window and sucked in a worried breath. Posy wasn't there any more. And neither was the vase of flowers.

The door took a while to open, as though whoever had been rushing to answer the bell had been distracted.

Eventually, Janie came to let them in, smiling but looking a bit stressed. William was standing behind her, clutching a rather wet kitten.

I was looking for you, Posy told Molly, her whiskers dripping. *It was a very good place to watch from, in front of those flowers. I could see everyone coming up and down the road. But then I forgot they were there.*

Molly stroked her damp fur and

Posy purred. A few little silvery sparks shimmered up between Molly's fingers, and she blinked. Hopefully no one else had noticed. William was looking at Kitty taking off her wellies. "Be careful," she whispered to Posy.

"She knocked the vase over!" William said, nodding. "Posy's not very good at being careful. But it didn't break. Kitty, come and see my cars!" He hurried off, still holding Posy, and Kitty followed him.

Janie sighed. "He's right, it didn't break. I think we've only got unbreakable vases left after nearly four years of William."

"She's a bit accident-prone, then,

your new kitten?" Mum asked as they went into the living room. Kitty and William were on the floor with the cars, and Posy was standing in a large red trailer that went with William's tractor. She looked nervous. When she saw Molly, she took a careful leap on to the floor and hurried over to weave around Molly's legs.

"Posy!" William sighed. "You were going to be the animals for the farm."

"I'm not sure she likes the trailer," Molly told him. "It's a bit wobbly."

Much too wobbly! Posy agreed.

"What about using Kitty's elephant instead?" Molly suggested. "Then the tractor could be a zoo tractor."

40

Kitty held up her elephant hopefully. She'd brought it with her from her box of toy animals from home. The elephant was her favourite. William thought about it for a moment, and nodded.

Posy gave a little purr of relief and climbed happily into Molly's lap. Molly looked round. Mum and Janie had gone into the kitchen, talking about nursery, and Kitty and William were busy with their game now, rolling the tractor all round the room and out into the hallway. No one would notice if she whispered to Posy.

"How's your tail?"

"Oh, it doesn't hurt. Although I think maybe that's why I knocked the vase over." Posy nodded. "It's put my balance off."

Molly had a feeling it was just that Posy had bumped into the vase, but it seemed mean to say so.

"I was thinking, maybe we should try and find out what your magic does. I'm sure it's useful for something."

Posy lay down flat with her paws stretched out in front of her and her chin on Molly's leg. Even her ears drooped. "Are you? I'm not. Perhaps I'm just no good at magic."

She sounded so sad that Molly picked her up, cuddling the kitten against her shoulder. Posy gave a squeak of surprise and then rubbed her chin against Molly's. "We'll work it out, I know we will," Molly whispered to her.

Posy purred, and the sound was so deep and lovely that it made Molly's hair shiver. "You promise?"

Molly nodded. "I promise." She wasn't sure how they'd do it, but Posy's purr had shimmered all through her. Molly felt as though even her fingernails were glittering.

With that much magic in such a small kitten, they had to be able to find something special that Posy was meant to do.

Chapter Four
The Lost Elephant

Molly sat dreamily in the corner
of the living room, surrounded by
William's toys, with Posy snuggled
into the hollow under her chin.
Molly's eyes were half-closed as
Posy's magic wrapped itself around
her like a gorgeous shimmering scarf.

She was woken out of her
daydream by a sudden howl from
Kitty.

"My elephant! I can't find him! Mummy, where's my elephant?" Kitty stood in the doorway, wailing loudly, her eyes filling with tears.

Molly's mum came in from the kitchen and followed Kitty out into the hallway.

"It's probably just under another of the toys," Molly heard her saying gently. "Don't worry, Kitty."

Molly went back to stroking Posy, but a couple of minutes later, Mum led Kitty back into the living room, still crying. William was following them, looking worried. Janie was still in the kitchen, making the tea.

"You haven't found it yet?" Molly asked, frowning. Kitty loved that elephant – she usually took it to bed with her.

Kitty shook her head. "William put it somewhere." Her voice was wobbly.

"It ran away from the zoo," William muttered. "But I can't remember where." He went back out into the hallway, and Molly could hear him rooting through his toys. Her mum hurried after him – it sounded as though he was looking underneath by simply flinging them all up in the air.

Kitty sat down next to Molly and leaned on her. "I might never find my elephant. . ." she whispered with a sniff. "He'll miss me."

47

Molly hugged her carefully, trying not to squash Posy. "I'll help you look too."

Molly felt Posy wriggle excitedly against her shoulder. *I can find it! I'm sure I can. I'm ever so good at finding things.* She stalked down Molly's arm to the floor and set off around the room, her ears laid back and her nose to the ground.

Kitty looked up at Molly, wide-eyed. "Is Posy looking for my elephant?"

Molly hesitated. Kitty didn't know about her magic, but her little sister loved animals too. Even if she did always want to dress them up. And right now, anything that made Kitty feel better was a good idea.

She nodded and whispered to Kitty. "Yes. But I wouldn't tell Mum. It's a special secret."

"I promise!" Kitty breathed, her eyes wide and miraculously emptied of tears now. "She's so clever!"

Molly and Kitty giggled as they watched Posy search, her tail swishing from side to side. The kitten was concentrating so hard on sniffing her way along the carpet that she walked straight into the sofa, and then sat down, looking cross with herself and shaking her head as though her nose hurt.

"Poor Posy!" Kitty patted her gently. "Please keep looking!" she whispered. "He's grey, and he's got a long trunk. His nose thing."

Posy looked up at Molly. *Oh good. I wasn't actually sure what an elephant was*, she admitted. She stood up and prowled out into the hallway. Mum and William had gone into the kitchen now, and Molly could hear a banging of pans, as though William was emptying out the kitchen cupboards in search of Kitty's elephant.

Posy stuck her nose into a corner

under the stairs and backed out sneezing, little delicate snorty sneezes, that made Kitty laugh. "She's the cleverest kitten *ever*," she told Molly. "How will she know where my elephant is?"

Molly shrugged her shoulders and smiled. "Magic," she whispered, and Kitty nodded, wide-eyed. "I thought so!"

It's dusty under there! Posy complained. *But I'm close, I'm sure of it. It's here somewhere.*

Molly crouched down beside her as Posy sniffed along the hall floor. "They were playing here," she whispered. "It would make sense."

I know it's here. I can feel your little

sister. Posy looked up at Kitty, who was staring at her hopefully, her blue eyes filling her face, they were so wide. *She needs it back, doesn't she? Some things belong to people so much that you feel it. The elephant wants her back too.*

Molly blinked in surprise. Kitty had said her elephant would miss her, but Molly hadn't realized it was true. Maybe it was. Perhaps Kitty had loved the elephant so much, he really belonged, and he knew he was lost. He was calling Posy to find him.

Oooh! Posy purred excitedly, her tail sticking straight up in the air like a furry flag. *We're close, we're close!* She was nosing through the neat line of shoes and wellies standing by the front door. William's were green with dinosaurs on, and Molly and Kitty had left theirs next to his, Molly's pawprint purple ones and Kitty's pink, scattered with little red hearts.

Posy stood up on her back paws, peering into the tops of the wellies. But she wasn't quite tall enough. With a little mew of crossness, she jumped, so suddenly that Molly gasped, "Careful!"

Kitty squeaked as the tabby kitten swayed on the top of Molly's purple welly boot.

Posy teetered nervously, hanging on the edge and wobbling; then she disappeared half inside the boot, so only her bottom was sticking out.

There was a strangled sort of meow, and her back end wriggled but didn't budge.

I've found it, she told Molly triumphantly. Then there was a little pause. *But I'm stuck*, she added. *Help!* And her tail flailed anxiously from side to side.

Molly was trying very hard not to laugh. She knew Posy would hate it if she did, but the twitching tabby bottom sticking out of the welly was just so funny.

Very gently, she tipped the welly a little and eased Posy out. The kitten came out backwards in a flurry of striped fur, and sat down immediately to swipe a paw across her nose and ears. She looked embarrassed, but she perked up when Kitty tipped the welly further and the grey toy elephant shot out. Kitty hugged it delightedly. "She found it! Posy found my elephant!" she cried. Then she looked at Molly and put her hand over her mouth in horror.

William and his mum and Molly's mum came out into the hallway, looking relieved.

"Posy tipped my wellies over by accident," Molly said quickly. "And Kitty's elephant was in one of them!"

William smiled suddenly. "Oh! I remember now. It just fitted." He nodded happily, and then looked a little shamefaced as everyone glared at him.

"Oh well." Molly's mum shook her head. "At least we've found it now. Thanks, Posy!" She leaned down and patted Posy gently.

Molly and Kitty smiled at each other, a secret little smile, and Posy purred happily. *I told you I was good at finding things,* she reminded Molly smugly. *I feel much better now.*

Molly nodded, and then she wrinkled her nose as a sudden thought came to her. Maybe this was Posy's magic? All that curious cleverness that kept getting her into trouble – it was because she was a finding kitten!

Chapter Five

Practising Magic

After tea, Kitty and William wanted to watch television, and Molly sat with them, with Posy lying on the sofa arm next to her.

I'm sure your magic is for finding things, Molly said in her mind to Posy.

Posy blinked and looked up at her questioningly.

How else could you be so good at searching? Molly asked.

So what should I do? Posy asked, her whiskers twitching. *Should I go out and look for things that are lost?*

Molly said nothing for a moment as she thought things through. *People lose things all the time. Now you know what to do, I'm sure it won't be long before you can use your magic again.*

Posy yawned and stretched out her front paws. *I want to use it now...* she told Molly, sounding sad and a little bit grumpy.

Molly frowned. It was being bored and having nothing to use her magic for that kept getting Posy into trouble. She needed something to keep her busy. Then Molly smiled.

I know. Grandad showed me a game, one that you'll love, Posy. Just close your eyes a minute, OK? Molly reached over to the little table next to the sofa and picked up a few little oddments – a pencil, one of Kitty's hairslides, a pair of scissors, a toy car and a piece of William's Lego. She arranged them on the sofa cushions between her and Posy, and then told

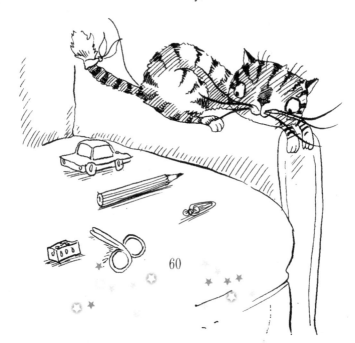

the kitten, *Now you can look! But only for a minute, Posy, and then you have to remember them all.*

Posy wriggled down the sofa arm so that she was almost vertical, with her paws just touching the cushions. *I like this game! I can remember them all already.*

Sure? Molly asked, pulling her school jumper over the objects so Posy couldn't see.

Posy nodded. She closed her eyes, and her whiskers sparkled, little glittery lights jumping from whisker to whisker, so that she glowed. Molly leaned closer, to hide her from Kitty and William, and Posy recited the list perfectly.

Wow. You're much better than me and Kitty, Molly told her.

Let's do it again! Posy pleaded. *I can feel it making my magic work really hard. It's lovely!*

"Time to go home, girls." Molly's mum put her head round the door. "Sorry!" she added, as Kitty began to protest. "It's late. Dad will be cooking our dinner by now."

Don't worry, Molly told Posy, as they went out into the hallway. *I've got a plan. You're allowed out into the* garden, aren't you? We walk past here on the way to school, so I'll find some more things and drop them over your fence when Mum isn't looking. Then you can play the game yourself.

When they got home, Molly searched out a bagful of odd bits from her bedroom and tucked them away inside her school bag. She was sure that practising with the game would help Posy keep her magic under control and stop her being quite so curious all the time.

The next morning, she trailed a little behind Mum and Kitty as they went down the lane on the way to school. As they came up to William's house, she saw Posy in her favourite spot in the window – it looked as though Janie had given up keeping a vase of flowers on the window sill.

Posy was gazing hopefully out across the front garden, and as she saw Molly, she stood up excitedly, patting her paws against the glass. Molly could see her little pink tongue and hear just a hint of a  mew through the window.

Molly waved to her and then looked round. Mum and Kitty weren't looking. Quickly, she dropped the little bag into the bushes on the other side of the fence, and pointed meaningfully at it. Posy immediately jumped down from the window sill, and Molly guessed that she was heading for her cat flap.

Over the next couple of days, Molly was careful to look at William's house on the way to school and back. She wasn't quite sure what she was looking for. There was never any sign of an accident caused by a nosy kitten. And Posy certainly hadn't been back to the vet's; Molly kept checking with her dad. Hopefully the game she'd made up for Posy was keeping her out of trouble.

That weekend, Molly was just wondering whether she could convince Kitty that she wanted to go and play with William so that they could see Posy again when her mum announced that actually, William was coming to Molly and Kitty's house that afternoon.

"I was saying to Janie that it was our turn to have William over, and she asked if it could be this weekend. They're trying to do some decorating and she's a bit worried about him getting into things... Apparently he got up at four o'clock this morning and tried to start painting his bedroom himself."

Molly nodded. She could just

imagine William and a large pot of paint. It put an end to her hopes of seeing Posy, though, which was sad. She sighed. William and a pot of paint was bad enough, but what about Posy? Molly chewed her bottom lip. She just hoped that Posy was enjoying playing her game. Otherwise, there would be painty kitten footprints all over William's house.

Mum knew William well enough to want to keep him out of the house as much as possible, so as soon as he arrived, she encouraged him and Kitty to go and play in the paddock behind the old farmhouse. It was a bright, sunny day, even though it was still freezing outside. It had been raining so much over the last few weeks that Molly decided she would go out too.

Kitty and William were playing a pirate game that seemed to Molly to be mostly just running around in circles, but it definitely had very complicated rules, as they kept having to stop and work out whether they were doing it properly or not.

Whoever had got it wrong had to walk the plank, with loud screams.

Molly sat on the fence between the paddock and the orchard and watched them for a while, but it was too cold for sitting still, so she wandered back inside. She had homework, unfortunately, and Mum made a fuss if she left it until the last minute.

Luckily, the history worksheet turned out to be really easy, so it was only about half an hour later when Molly went back downstairs, planning to ask Mum for a snack.

"Shall I get Kitty and William and see if they want some?" she asked, as her mum searched in the cupboard for some biscuits.

Her mum nodded. "Yes, please, Molly. I was outside with those two and I was just thinking about getting everyone a snack, but the phone rang. I hope they're all right out there," she added, peering out of the kitchen window at the paddock. "I was on the phone a little while." She frowned. "Well, Kitty looks as if she's in one piece. I can't see William."

"I'll call them." Molly ran out into the yard and round the side of the house. "Kitty! Bring William back in for a snack. Mum's got biscuits."

Kitty raced towards her at once, and Molly hurried back inside. It

was far too cold to be out without a
coat.

"Where's William?" Mum asked, as
Kitty burst in, aiming for the plate
of biscuits. "And take your boots
off!"

Kitty sighed and sat down on the
floor to take her wellies off. "Are
they chocolate ones?"

"Yes. Kitty, doesn't William want
a snack? He should probably come
in anyway, it's cold out there." Mum
looked out at the paddock. It was
getting late now, and the bright sun
had gone in, leaving a dingy, greyish
afternoon. "Kitty, where *is* William?"
Mum asked, her voice suddenly
anxious.

71

"I don't know." Kitty bit into her biscuit. "He walked the plank and a sea monster ate him."

Chapter Six
The Finding Kitten

Kitty went on eating her biscuit while Molly and her mum stared at her. Then Molly's mum raced outside, calling anxiously for William.

"Kitty!" Molly crouched down next to her sister and looked her in the eyes, very seriously. "Kitty, there isn't really any such thing as sea monsters. Where did William go?"

Kitty scowled, but then she looked down, as though she didn't want to meet Molly's eyes. "He went away ... because I poked him with my sword."

"Sword?"

"It was only a stick. He did it to me too!" Kitty complained. "*I* didn't start crying and run away."

"I can't see him anywhere..." Mum came back in looking really worried.

"They had an argument and William went off somewhere," Molly told her.

"Where, Kitty?" Mum asked. "Did he go home? Janie hasn't called me to say he's turned up."

"Don't know," Kitty muttered. She looked sulky. "He's not my friend any more."

"Kitty, William might be lost," Mum said. She was trying not to sound too upset, Molly could tell. She didn't want to scare Kitty. But her voice was a bit wobbly with worry. "Please try and think which way he went."

"He's not lost..." Kitty looked up, her eyes suddenly wide. "He was cross. He went away!" She stood up and looked around the kitchen anxiously as though she thought William might appear out of one of the cupboards. (Which wasn't such a silly idea, knowing William.) "He's not lost, is he?" she asked, her voice quavering like Mum's had.

Lost? Molly thought at once of Posy – she would be able to help find William! Molly blinked, and

turned slowly to look at the kitchen door, which Mum had left open when she ran back in.

A small stripy tabby face was peering around the edge of the door. Posy's whiskers were shimmering already, and she was looking hopefully at Molly.

I could hear something was wrong, all the way down the lane! Something very important must be lost, Molly. I've been practising with your bag of things. Please can I help?

Molly nodded, but put a finger to her lips to remind Posy to be careful in front of Mum and Kitty.

"I'm going to look round the paddock," she told Mum, who was still trying to get Kitty to tell her exactly what had happened.

"All right." Mum smiled at her distractedly. "Thanks, Molly."

Molly put her coat on and hurried out, with Posy twirling around her feet excitedly, nearly tripping her up. Molly noticed that there was a splash of yellow paint on the tip of her tail – as if she'd tried to join in the decorating.

What are we looking for? Posy demanded. *Why were your mum and your little sister so upset?*

"We can't find William," Molly explained, looking anxiously at Posy.

My William? Posy sounded horrified.

"Yes! I'm really sorry. He and Kitty got into a fight about their game..."

Posy nodded, as though she wasn't that surprised. *He ran away?*

"Yes, and we don't know where. Can you feel him, Posy?"

The kitten looked around, her glowing whiskers waving in the greyish afternoon light. Molly had never seen any other cat move its whiskers quite like that. It was as if they were tasting the air, searching for William.

I've never looked for a person before, she said uncertainly. *It's different. I'm not sure how. . .*

Molly swallowed, trying to sound calm and not panicky. "Perhaps if you think about William?" she suggested. "And then send your magic after him?"

Posy laid her ears back a little. *This morning he spilled a bowl of cornflakes on my head.*

"Oh..." It was probably because she was worried about William, but Molly wanted so much to laugh. She could just imagine Posy covered in cornflakes. "And milk?"

Yes. Actually, the cornflakes tasted quite nice.

"Could you think about cornflakes, then? And William's big red tractor? That's his favourite toy."

Posy sat down in the middle of the paddock, and Molly could almost feel her thinking. Her fur ruffled out so that it was all on end, and Molly remembered the day she'd first met Posy at the surgery. Then she hadn't known what to do with her magic. And now, hopefully...

Molly gave a little gasp. Posy was covered in sparkling silver magic now, like a little firework kitten. Her magic had grown so much stronger. Molly was sure her memory game had helped. Molly sniffed suddenly. She could smell cornflakes on the air, and sweet milk, and her hair felt suddenly sticky. A spell was working all around them...

Posy stood up and marched across the paddock. She was so little that she half-disappeared in the long frosty grass, and she could walk right underneath the orchard fence, without her tail-tip even touching it. Molly had to scramble over the top to follow her.

The orchard looked strange and ghostly now that it was getting dark – there was a thin mist weaving around the black trees, and it was very quiet.

"Are you sure?" Molly asked Posy, trying not to sound doubtful. "It's a bit frightening in here."

William likes frightening things, Posy pointed out. *Spiders. And dinosaurs. He plays with those a lot. They could live somewhere like this.*

Molly nodded. That was probably true. "But if he's only in the orchard, why didn't he come when Mum called him?"

Posy stopped, staring proudly up into one of the largest apple trees, one with long, curling branches that swept down almost to the ground. Right in the middle of the tree, snuggled up close to the trunk, was William.

He was cosily wrapped up in his big scarlet jacket, and gloves, and his woolly scarf, and he was fast asleep.

That's why, Posy said proudly. *I found him, Molly!*

Molly picked her up and hugged her. "You're so clever! You're a star, Posy." She giggled. "I suppose it's tiring being eaten by a sea monster." She turned, hurrying back through the trees to the fence. "Mum! Mum! I've found him!"

Molly leaned on the fence, watching her mum and Kitty racing towards them, and dabbed a light little kiss on Posy's soft head. "Well done, Posy. That was brilliant magic."

Posy purred, and slipped out of Molly's arms like a tiny grey shadow, heading back home.

I know. . .

www.holly-webb.com
www.scholastic.co.uk/zone

HOLLY WEBB loves the idea of
World Book Day – a whole day
that's all about reading!

Her dream job as a child was to be
a librarian, so she could sit in the library
and read everything. She never thought
about being a writer, she was a reader.
Books were the ultimate adventure for a
shy child who wasn't very good at
running fast or climbing things.

It wasn't until Holly was much older
that she discovered the pleasure of writing,
too. Now Holly loves the thought that
people are curled up with one of her
books, imagining themselves into another
world. (Though she thinks running and
climbing are great too. Books are even
better read halfway up a tree!)

Holly lives in Reading with her
husband, three sons and a cat who isn't
quite as troublesome as Posy.

WORLD
BOOK
DAY

1 MARCH 2012

Want to **WIN** a year's supply of **BOOKS** for you and your school?

Of course you do ...

This is one of our favourite books (that's why it's in our **HALL OF FAME**!), but we want to know what *your* favourite book is (or *your* favourite character – whether it's the baddest baddie or the superest hero)!

It's that easy to win, so visit
WWW.WORLDBOOKDAY.COM now!